The full-color photographs were reproduced from 35-mm slides.
The text type is Kabel Medium.
Copyright © 1998 by Miela Ford
http://www.williammorrow.com
Printed in Hong Kong by South China Printing Company (1988) Ltd.
First Edition 10 9 8 7 6 5 4 3 2 1

Library of Congress Cataloging-in-Publication Data
Ford, Miela.
Watch us play / by Miela Ford.
    p.   cm.
Summary: Two lion cubs in the zoo frolic with each
other until they are ready to take a nap.
ISBN 0-688-15606-1 (trade).   ISBN 0-688-15607-X (lib. bdg.)
[1. Lions—Fiction.   2. Zoo animals—Fiction.]   I. Title.
PZ7.F75322Wat   1998   [E]—dc21   97-6948   CIP   AC

WATCH US Pl

PICTURES AND WORDS BY

MIELA FORD

GREENWILLOW BOOKS NEW YORK

For Jeneva
and her
students

Hey, Dad, look at me!

Hey, Mom, look at me!

We're ready now.

Watch us play.

On my back.

Touch my toes.

Peek-a-boo.

I see you.

Tease

and tickle.

Tag

a tail.

Find a stick

and share it.

We've played enough.

Now we're done.

Hey, Mom! Hey, Dad!

Watch us nap.